Pink Princess
Rules the School

by Alyssa Crowne

illustrated by Charlotte Alder

Scholastic Inc.

New York   Toronto   London   Auckland
Sydney   Mexico City   New Delhi   Hong Kong

For Susan,

who gave me the magic key
that unlocked the heart of this story.

No part of this publication may be reproduced, stored in a
retrieval system, or transmitted in any form or by any means,
electronic, mechanical, photocopying, recording, or otherwise,
without written permission of the publisher. For information
regarding permission, write to Scholastic Inc, Attention:
Permissions Department, 557 Broadway, New York, NY 10012.

ISBN: 978-0-545-21173-4

Text copyright © 2009 by Pure West Productions, Inc.
Illustrations copyright © 2009 by Scholastic Inc.

All rights reserved. Published by Scholastic Inc.

SCHOLASTIC, LITTLE APPLE, PERFECTLY PRINCESS,
and associated logos are trademarks and/or
registered trademarks of Scholastic Inc.

12 11 10 9 8 7 6 5 4 3 2   10 11 12 13 14 15/0

Designed by Kevin Callahan
First trade printing, February 2010

Contents

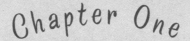

Chapter One

A Present for a Princess

Juliet marched around her pink bedroom. She held her favorite doll, Princess Allissa, high above her head. Princess Allissa and Juliet both had long blonde hair and blue eyes. Princess Allissa wore a pink gown. Juliet wore a pink shirt and pink jeans.

Juliet turned to face a row of stuffed animals and dolls on her bookshelf. She talked in her best, most royal princess voice.

"Hello, my loyal subjects," Juliet said loudly. She moved Princess Allissa's head back and forth.

Her loyal subjects were a teddy bear, stuffed frog, and fairy doll. They stared at her.

"I have a . . . a . . ." Juliet knew there was a word that meant a princess had something important to say. But she couldn't remember it.

"I have something to say," she said instead. "From now on, everything in our kingdom will be pink!"

Juliet ran to the bookshelf. She picked up the teddy bear.

"Hooray! I love pink!" she said in the teddy bear's low voice.

She picked up the frog next. "Pink is the best color ever!" croaked the frog.

Then the fairy doll spoke. "Princess Allissa is a great princess!"

Juliet had Princess Allissa give a bow. "Thank you! Thank you!"

Then Juliet's mom called from the kitchen. "Juliet! Please come here!"

Juliet put Princess Allissa in her toy castle and ran downstairs.

"Mom," she said, "what's that word for when a princess says something important?"

Juliet's mom wrinkled her nose. She always did that when she was thinking hard.

"You mean a decree?" she asked.

Juliet nodded. "That's it! A royal decree. Thanks." She started to go back upstairs, but her mom stopped her.

"Juliet, a package came for you," said her mom. "It's from Aunt Maxine."

"For me?" Juliet asked. She ran up to the box on the kitchen table. The label said *Juliet Henry.* It *was* for her!

She tried to open the box, but it was taped shut.

"I'll help you," her mom said. Mrs. Henry cut through the tape with scissors. Juliet bounced up and down on her toes, waiting for her mom to finish.

Inside was another box wrapped in pink paper. A card was taped to it.

"It's a present!" Juliet cried.

"Aunt Maxine is early," her mom said. "Your birthday is still two weeks away."

"I don't mind," Juliet said. She ripped the pink paper.

"Juliet! The card first, please," her mom told her.

Juliet made a face. Parents always wanted you to open the card first. They made you wait *forever* to get your present. But that was the best part!

The card had a big pink number 7 on it and lots of glitter. Inside was a message from Aunt Maxine. Juliet read it out loud.

"*Dear Princess Juliet,*
I am sorry I can't come
to your Princess Party.
Here is a present you can
use at your party.
I hope you like it.
    Have a happy birthday!
    Love,
    Aunt Maxine"

"It's something for the party," Juliet said. She ripped the pink paper again. "I wonder what it is."

Under the paper was a plain white box. Juliet lifted the lid and gasped.

"It's a crown!" she cried.

She picked up the crown. It was gold,

with pink jewels all around it. It felt heavy, like a real crown.

"It's just like Princess Allissa's crown," she said.

"It will match your pink dress perfectly," her mom added. "You know, I've been thinking about the party. Last year you invited all of the boys and girls in your class. Are you sure you don't want to invite the boys this time?"

"Just girls," Juliet said firmly. "You can't have boys at a Princess Party. That's just silly."

Juliet ran to the mirror in the hall. She put the crown on her head. It was the most beautiful crown she had ever seen!

"Princess Juliet," she whispered.

Juliet's mom gave her a kiss on the cheek. "You look like a real princess. Now let's put the crown back in the box. We should keep it safe until the party."

But Juliet put both of her hands on the crown and held it to her head. "Oh, no!" she said. "We can't put it away. I'm going to wear it to school on Monday!"

Chapter Two

Trouble on the Bus

On Monday morning, Juliet got ready for school. She pulled on her favorite jeans with pink flowers on the pockets. Her white shirt had matching pink flowers. Juliet put on her pink shoes. Finally, she placed the gold crown on top of her head.

"Juliet, are you sure you want to wear that to school?" her mom asked. Mrs. Henry was frowning.

Juliet's mom and dad were getting ready

for work. Her mom worked in an office. She always wore a jacket and skirt and her fancy pearl necklace. Juliet's dad was a cook. He wore a white coat and black and white striped pants.

Mr. Henry was packing Juliet's lunch into her pink lunch bag. "I think the crown looks very nice," he said.

"Yes, it does," her mom agreed. "But I don't think school is a good place to wear a crown."

"Why not?" Juliet asked. "Jonathan always wears a baseball cap."

"I know, but—" Mrs. Henry looked at the clock. "Oh, I'm late. Have a nice day, sweetie." She gave Juliet a kiss on the cheek and ran out the door.

Juliet's dad strapped a sparkly backpack onto Juliet's back. "I can hear the bus," he said. "I'll see you later, Princess."

"Bye, Dad!"
Juliet waved as she
ran out the door.

The yellow
school bus pulled
up in front of
her house. The
door squeaked
open and Juliet
climbed on
board. Kids
were talking and
laughing. The bus was almost full.

Juliet didn't have to worry about finding a seat. She always sat next to her best friend, Olivia.

"Oh, Juliet, I love your crown!" Olivia said. Olivia had shiny brown hair that came down to her chin. Today, she wore a green T-shirt with a monkey on it.

Juliet sat down. "Thanks," she said. "My aunt Maxine gave it to me. It's for my birthday."

Billy Walker leaned over the seat behind them.

"What's on your head, Juliet?" he asked. "Is that an alien space helmet?"

"Of course not," Juliet said in her most royal voice. "It's a princess crown."

"Ha!" Billy laughed. "You can't wear a princess crown to school."

Juliet turned around and looked over the seat.

Billy's friend Jonathan Kim sat next to him, wearing his red baseball cap, like always. Juliet thought Jonathan was nice. She didn't know why he was friends with a mean boy like Billy.

"Jonathan wears a baseball cap," she said. "If he can wear a cap, then I can wear a crown."

"Jonathan plays baseball," Billy shot
back. "So he's allowed to wear a cap. But
you're not a real princess!"

"How do you know I'm not a princess?"
Juliet asked. She sometimes thought she
might be. It happened all the time in
stories. Girls grew up in normal houses.

Then, *bam!* One day a fairy godmother showed up and said you were a princess.

Olivia joined in. "Juliet can wear a crown if she wants to."

"No, she can't," Billy said. "A crown is a costume. You can only wear costumes on Halloween."

"It is *not* a costume!" Juliet said loudly. "It is a fashion accessory."

Billy made a face. "Girls are so weird," he said to Jonathan.

Juliet turned back around. She folded her arms in front of her. Billy Walker made her so angry!

"He's mean," Olivia whispered.

"He's not even mean," Juliet said. "He's just jealous. I bet he wishes he had a crown as good as mine!"

Chapter Three

Princess Juliet's Decree

All of the girls in Juliet's class made a fuss over her crown. Juliet let them try it on as they waited in line to go into school.

"I got it for my Princess Party," Juliet explained. "Everyone's invited."

"Am I invited?" Billy asked. He tried to grab the crown from Juliet's hand. She pulled it away from him and put it back on her head.

"No, you are not," she said. "No boys allowed. Especially you!"

Billy got a mad look on his face. The bell rang, and the kids all went into their classroom. Their teacher, Mrs. Masters, was waiting for them.

Juliet thought Mrs. Masters was the nicest teacher ever. She reminded Juliet of a fairy godmother. Her silvery gray hair was very curly. She liked to wear sparkly jewelry. Juliet knew Mrs. Masters would love her crown.

She was right. "That's a very nice crown you have on, Juliet," Mrs. Masters said.

"Thank you," Juliet replied, giving Mrs. Masters a big smile.

For most of the morning, Juliet forgot that she was even wearing her crown. The day started out with story time. Mrs. Masters read a funny story about a dog. Then they learned the spelling words for the week.

After snack, it was map time. Mrs.

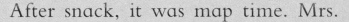

Masters had a big map in the front of the room. Every Monday, she talked about a different place on the map. Students could point out a place on the map, too.

"Would anyone like to go to the map today?" Mrs. Masters asked.

Juliet raised her hand.

"Yes, Juliet," Mrs. Masters said.

Juliet sat in the back of the room. She liked it there, because when she went up to the board she got to walk down the aisle between the desks. She always imagined she was a princess walking through her castle. Juliet kept her back straight when she walked, just like a princess would. In her mind, she gave a little princess wave. Her loyal subjects clapped and cheered for her.

"Look at her alien space helmet!" Billy called out. All of the boys in the class laughed with him.

Juliet's face turned red. So much for her loyal subjects.

"Billy, that's not nice," Mrs. Masters said sternly. "Juliet, please go on."

Juliet pointed to a state on the map.

"This is California. My aunt Maxine lives here," Juliet said. "She's the one who sent me my crown."

"I have a friend who lives in the California desert," Mrs. Masters said. "It's very hot there."

Juliet went back to her seat. Billy was still laughing when she walked by, so she made sure not to look at him.

Soon it was time for lunch. Juliet and the girls in her class sat together at one big, long table. Some girls brought lunch from home, like Juliet. Others got hot lunch from the cafeteria kitchen. The boys sat at a table next to them.

All of the girls were excited about Juliet's birthday party.

"What are you going to wear, Juliet?" asked Hannah. She had long brown hair.

"I think she'll wear something pink," said Kristen. "You're crazy about pink, Juliet. I bet you'll have a pink house when you grow up, and a pink car, and maybe even a pink dog."

Kristen had curly blonde hair. She always made Juliet laugh.

"I do have a pink dress," Juliet said. "I can't wait to wear it!"

"I wish your party was tomorrow!" Kristen sighed.

"Me, too," Olivia agreed. "What are we going to do? Will there be games, like last year?"

Juliet nodded. "Yes. And crafts. We're going to make princess crowns."

"*Oooooh!*" said all of the girls at once.

"How can we wait two whole weeks?" Hannah asked.

Juliet was feeling even more excited than when she got her crown. She didn't want to wait for her party, either!

Just then, an idea popped into her head.

She stood up. "I have a royal decree! From now on, every day is princess day. Tomorrow, all princesses will wear pink to school!"

The girls giggled.

"What's a decree?" Hannah asked.

"It means we have to do it," Olivia told her.

Hannah nodded. "Okay. It sounds like fun!"

All the girls said they would wear pink. Juliet smiled.

Tomorrow, princesses would rule the lunchroom.

Soon, they would rule the school!

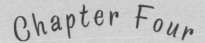

Chapter Four

Ten Pink Princesses

That night, Juliet told her parents all about the princess plan as they ate dinner.

"So all of the girls are going to wear pink tomorrow?" her mom asked.

"Yes," Juliet said. "All of them."

"What if some of them don't like pink?" her mom asked. "My favorite color is blue."

"They all like it," Juliet said. It was a guess, but she was pretty sure. Who didn't like pink?

"I guess you'll see tomorrow," said Juliet's dad. "I know you'll wear pink. You have so many pink clothes, you could wear pink every day!"

The next day, the students filed into Mrs. Masters's class. They took off their jackets, and Juliet smiled. All ten girls were wearing pink!

Olivia wore a pink shirt with hearts on it. Hannah had on a pink skirt and a white T-shirt. Kristen wore pink pants with polka dots on them, and pink sunglasses, too. The rest of the girls all had on at least one pink thing.

Juliet had on more pink than anybody else. She wore her pink pants and pink T-shirt. Her socks and sneakers were pink. She even wore pink beads around her neck.

"The pink princesses are here!" Juliet cheered.

Billy Walker put his hands over his eyes. He fell to his knees.

"Help! All that pink is hurting my eyes!" he cried.

The other boys laughed. They clapped their hands over their eyes, too. Even Jonathan!

"Help! Help us!" the boys yelled. "Too much pink!"

Juliet put her hands on her hips. "Well, it hurts *my* eyes to look at your boring blue shirt, Billy!"

Mrs. Masters walked up to them. "Please settle down," she said. "There are many different colors in the world. No color is better than another."

"Especially not pink," Billy grumbled.

"That's enough, Billy," Mrs. Masters said. "Class, please sit down."

Juliet couldn't wait until lunch. Then the princesses would rule the lunchroom! She thought about princesses all morning.

Finally, it was time for lunch. Juliet stood in the hot lunch line first. She hadn't brought food because today was her favorite hot lunch: macaroni and cheese. Juliet took a carton of milk and a salad, too.

Soon, all ten pink princesses sat around the table. Juliet put down her tray.

"Let the princess lunch begin!" she said.

"What do we do?" Hannah asked.

Juliet hadn't really thought it all out. Wearing pink clothes was as far as she had gotten.

"Well, we eat our princess lunch," she said, shrugging.

Kristen stuck a fork in her macaroni and cheese. "Mmm, princess macaroni!" she said.

Hannah made a face. "Princesses don't eat macaroni and cheese!"

"Of course they do," Juliet said. "It's delicious. Princesses eat things that are delicious."

Hannah shook her head. "Princesses eat things like little cakes and flower petals."

Down the table, some of the other girls were whispering. "I think that's what fairies eat," Jin said.

"But maybe princesses eat that stuff, too," Malia added.

Juliet didn't like how this was going. They were supposed to be acting like princesses. Instead, they were talking about macaroni and cheese.

Then Olivia spoke up.

"We can pretend," she said. She pointed

to her plate. "The macaroni and cheese is made of gold. The salad is made of flower petals."

Juliet was so glad Olivia was her best friend. She always had good ideas.

Juliet held up her milk carton. "And this is a goblet of water from a magical fountain!" she added.

Kristen took a sip of her milk. "Ah, this tastes very magical!" she said.

The girls giggled. Juliet was glad. Everyone started acting like princesses.

"Are you going to the princess ball tomorrow night?" Jin asked Malia in a fancy princess voice.

"Yes," Malia said. "But I don't have anything to wear! I hope my fairy godmother brings me a dress."

Pretending was fun, but Juliet had another idea. She waited until everyone was done eating.

"I have another royal decree," Juliet said. "Tomorrow, we will all wear pink again. We will also bring pink food!"

Jin and Malia whispered to each other again. "Where are we going to get pink food?" Jin asked, after a minute.

"Lots of food is pink," Juliet said. "I eat pink food all the time, like strawberry yogurt. And strawberry jelly sandwiches, and strawberry milk."

"And strawberries," Kristen added.

"Raspberries are pink, too," Olivia pointed out.

"See?" Juliet said. "Pink food is easy."

Juliet couldn't wait until tomorrow. It was going to be the best princess day ever!

Chapter Five

Pirates Versus Princesses

Juliet hopped off the bus and ran into her house. Her dad was already home, making dinner.

"Dad! Dad! Can we bake pink cookies tonight?" Juliet asked.

"Slow down, Princess," her dad said. He helped pull her backpack off of her back. "Sure, we can make cookies. Is there a bake sale?"

"No," Juliet said. "All the girls are bringing pink food for lunch tomorrow.

I need a pink sandwich, too. And pink milk."

"Hmm, let me guess," Mr. Henry said. "Was this your idea?"

Juliet smiled wide. "Of course!"

Her dad shook his head. "I think I will have to call you the *Pink* Princess from now on."

The Pink Princess. Juliet liked the sound of that.

Mr. Henry walked to the kitchen table and held up a stack of pink paper.

"I got the paper for your party invitations," he said. "Are you sure you don't want to invite the boys? We have room for everyone. I thought you all had fun together last year."

Juliet shook her head hard. "The boys would spoil it. They don't even like pink. Billy says it hurts his eyes."

Her dad laughed. "It's your party," he

said, shrugging. "Mom and I will help you with the invitations."

"Thanks, Dad," Juliet said.

Juliet ran upstairs. Princess Allissa was resting in the bed in her princess castle. Juliet picked her up.

"Just wait, Allissa," she said. "Tomorrow, the Pink Princess will *really* rule the school!"

The next day, Juliet brought her pink lunch to school. She wore a pink dress. She had the cookies in her bag that she and her dad had baked.

On the bus, Juliet sat with Olivia. Behind them, Billy and Jonathan snickered.

Juliet turned around. "What's so funny?" she asked.

"Nothing," Billy said. "You'll see."

Billy and the other boys acted strange all morning. They didn't make

fun of pink,
or crack jokes
about Juliet's
crown. Instead,
they whispered
to one another.
They pointed
and laughed at the
girls when Mrs. Masters wasn't looking.
It made Juliet worry. What were they
planning?

The lunch bell finally rang, and Juliet
forgot all about the boys. It was time for
the pink princess lunch!

All the pink princesses settled in at the
lunch table.

"All right, princesses," Juliet said.
"Please show your pink princess food."

Olivia went first. "I have pink yogurt,"
she said.

"Me, too," Hannah chimed in.

Kristen had a cupcake with pink icing. Jin and Malia brought pink chips that tasted like shrimp. Emily and Taylor brought strawberry milk. Elena and Sandra had strawberries.

Juliet was proud of her pink lunch. She took each thing out of her lunch bag one at a time.

"I have a sandwich with cream cheese and pink jelly," Juliet said. "It's shaped like a heart. I also have pink yogurt and pink milk."

She paused, saving the best for last. "Now, feast your eyes on a royal treat. Pink cookies for everybody!"

Juliet opened the bag of pink cookies and held up a cookie shaped like a star. It had pink icing and shiny pink sprinkles.

"Ooooh!" the girls all cried.

"I have another royal decree," Juliet said, grinning. "Let's eat!"

Juliet took a bite of her sandwich. Then she heard a voice. It was *not* a lovely princess voice.

"Hand over your treasure!"

Billy and the other boys had surrounded the table! Billy had a patch on his eye, like a pirate. Some of the other boys wore patches, too. Jonathan had a bandana tied on his head.

"We're pirates," Billy said. "And pirates rob princesses! Now give us your treasure. *Aaargh!*"

"*Aaaargh!*" the boys all yelled. They shook their fists like pirates.

Juliet stood up and put her hands on her hips. "You *cannot* have any treasure, Billy!" she yelled. "We are playing princesses, not pirates. Leave us alone!"

"Oh, yeah?" Billy said. He reached across the table and swiped the bag of cookies!

Juliet tried to grab them back, but Billy was fast. He took the cookies to the boys' table. Juliet watched as he stuck his hand into the bag and shoved a cookie into his mouth.

"Aaargh!" he cried again, his mouth full. Cookie crumbs flew everywhere.

The other boys cheered and started eating the cookies, too.

"Mrs. Linda!" Juliet yelled the name of the lunch lady as loud as she could. But Hannah had already run to get her.

"What's wrong?" the lunch lady asked.

"The boys stole our cookies," Juliet said. She pointed right at Billy.

Mrs. Linda shook her head. "Let me take care of this."

Mrs. Linda talked to the boys for a minute. Then she and Billy came back to the girls' table. He wasn't wearing his eye patch.

"Billy has something to say," the lunch lady told the girls.

Billy looked at his sneakers. "I'm sorry we took your cookies," he mumbled.

Mrs. Linda gave the bag back to Juliet. The bag felt awfully light. Juliet opened it, starting to feel mad.

All of the beautiful cookies were gone! Only a few broken cookie pieces were left.

Juliet felt like crying. The princess lunch was ruined!

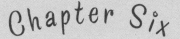

Chapter Six

No More Costumes

Juliet was in a bad mood when they got back to class.

Then her bad mood got worse.

Mrs. Masters had heard about what happened at lunch.

"Pretending is a good thing," she said to the class. "But this pretending is making girls and boys fight each other. That isn't good at all."

"But the girls weren't fighting!" Juliet

objected. "We were playing. The boys started it."

"Did not!" Billy shouted. "You started it by wearing your crown."

"That's not true!" Juliet yelled.

"I think the answer is simple," Mrs. Masters said, holding up her hands for silence. "Costumes are fun, but they don't belong in school. We need a new rule— no more costumes in class. No more pirate patches. No more princess crowns."

Juliet put a hand on her crown. "But it's not a costume. It's a fashion accessory!" she blurted out.

Juliet's eyes felt hot. She wanted to cry, but she did not want to cry in front of the class.

"I'm sorry, Juliet," Mrs. Masters said. "Please leave your crown at home from now on."

Juliet slowly took off her crown and put it inside her desk. She raised her hand again.

"Does that mean I can't wear pink anymore?" she asked when Mrs. Masters called on her.

Mrs. Masters smiled. "You can wear any color you want," she said.

Juliet felt a little better. She wanted to wear her crown. But she could still pretend to be a princess without it.

For the whole rest of the day, the kids in class were quiet. Nobody got in trouble.

On the bus that afternoon, Juliet wrote a note:

Wear pink tomorrow. Bring pink food. The pink princesses will not give up!

She folded up the note. On the front, she used a pink pencil to write, *For girls only. Pass it on.*

Olivia looked nervous. "I thought we couldn't play princesses anymore," she said.

"Mrs. Masters just said we couldn't wear costumes," Juliet said. "But we can still wear pink. She said so. And she didn't say anything about what we could eat."

Olivia frowned. Juliet passed the note to Jin and Malia. As she leaned across the bus aisle, Billy tapped her shoulder.

"What do you want?" Juliet asked. She did not want to talk to him.

"I *told* you your crown was a costume," Billy said. "Ha! I was right."

Juliet was in a bad mood all over again.

It wasn't fair. Billy and the boy pirates started the fight. Didn't Mrs. Masters know that pirates were mean, and princesses were nice? That's how it was in every story! Princesses should never get in trouble—just pirates.

Juliet was glad the boys weren't coming to her party. They didn't deserve to. In fact, she never wanted to talk to them again!

Chapter Seven

The End of Pink?

When Juliet got home, she stomped through the front door.

"Did you have a bad day?" her dad asked.

"I had the *worst* day!" Juliet said. "Pirates attacked us and now I can't wear my crown, even though the girls didn't do anything wrong."

"Slow down." Mr. Henry put a glass of milk on the kitchen table for Juliet. "Sit down and tell me the story from the start."

Juliet told her dad all about Billy and the pirates. Then she repeated what Mrs. Masters had said.

"It's not fair!" Juliet pouted.

"Tell you what," her dad said. "Tonight I'll make you more pink cookies. Okay?"

Juliet nodded. "But what about my crown? Maybe you can write a note to Mrs. Masters and tell her to let me wear it."

"I think your teacher's right," her dad said. "School might not be the best place to wear your crown. You can wear it here whenever you want. And at your party, of course."

Juliet frowned. "I'll ask Mom when she gets home."

"Your mom will say the same thing," Mr. Henry said. "Sorry, Princess."

Juliet knew her dad was right. But she still felt mad inside. She didn't want to give up.

When her mom came home from work, Juliet told her the whole story.

"So you can see that it's not fair," Juliet finished. "I should get to wear my crown."

"I think Mrs. Masters is right," her mom said. "School isn't a good place to wear a crown."

"That's just what Dad said!" Juliet took the crown from her backpack and stomped upstairs. She put the crown on her dresser, next to Princess Allissa.

"Princess Allissa, you will have to guard my crown while I'm at school," she said. "Bad pirates might steal it. Keep it safe."

She talked in Princess Allissa's voice. "Pirates are mean. And they look like they're smelly. If any pirates come around here, I will punish them."

Juliet picked up her stuffed frog. "Who wants to play pirates, anyway? That's so boring," she croaked in the frog's voice.

"You're so right, frog," Juliet said. "Playing princess is much better. Everybody knows that!"

Juliet still felt mad the next morning. She put on a pink skirt and shirt and her pink shoes. The crown still sat on her dresser.

"Sorry I can't wear you," she said sadly, leaving the room.

Downstairs, her dad gave her a white box with a pink ribbon on it.

"More cookies," he said. "See? They're pirate-proof."

Juliet hugged her dad. She felt a little less mad inside. They could have another princess lunch!

"Thank you," Juliet said.

Juliet skipped out to meet the bus. She plopped down next to Olivia. Billy and Jonathan sat quietly behind them.

"Look!" she told Olivia. "More cookies. We can have a princess lunch today."

"Great!" Olivia said. "Your dad makes the best cookies." Olivia was wearing a green soccer T-shirt and blue sweatshirt. She had on jeans and white sneakers.

Juliet frowned. "Why aren't you wearing pink?"

"Because I'm not," Olivia said.

"But you saw the note," Juliet said. "We need to wear pink today so we can play princess at lunch."

"I like playing princess," Olivia said. "But do I always have to wear pink? Yellow is my favorite color, anyway."

Juliet felt mad all over again. "You're taking sides with the boys!"

"I am not!" Olivia said.

"You are too!"

Juliet folded her arms. She didn't talk to Olivia for the rest of the bus ride.

How could they play princess if nobody wore pink?

Chapter Eight

The Trade

Olivia sat at the end of the table with Jin and Malia at lunch.

"Are we playing princesses?" Hannah asked. She had pink on her dress.

"I don't feel like it," Juliet said.

"What's in the box?" Kristen asked.

"Pink cookies," Juliet replied. "You can have some, if you want."

Hannah's eyes got wide. "What if the pirates steal them again?"

Kristen giggled. "I hope they do. That was fun!"

"It was *not* fun," Juliet said. She made her voice very loud. "And if any boys try to steal these cookies they will get in big trouble!"

She glanced over at Billy. He was looking down at his plate.

Juliet opened the box. "Here," she announced. "Princess cookies for everyone!"

Juliet ate the sandwich her dad had made for her. She sipped her strawberry milk.

After a few minutes, Jonathan walked up to the table. Juliet put down her milk and grabbed the box of cookies.

"Stop right there," she said, pulling the box close to her. "I will tell Mrs. Linda."

"I don't want to steal your cookies," Jonathan said. He held up a bag of chips. "I want to trade."

Juliet didn't know what to think. "Trade? Why?"

"Those were really good cookies," Jonathan said. "I'm sorry we stole them. We were just playing."

Juliet hugged the cookie box closer. "Are you sure you want a *pink* cookie?"

Jonathan shrugged. "Pink is okay. I like pink."

Juliet couldn't believe it. A boy liked pink?

"Then why did you boys make fun of it?" Juliet asked.

Jonathan shrugged. "I don't know. I guess Billy is mad at you."

"Why?" Juliet asked.

"Because he's not invited to your birthday party," Jonathan said. "Your party last year was fun."

Juliet thought about it. Her mom and dad kept saying that she should invite the boys. Maybe they were right.

Juliet gave Jonathan a cookie. He gave her the bag of chips.

"Thanks," he said.

Juliet smiled. She couldn't wait to get home. She had a new idea.

A really *big* idea!

Chapter Nine

Crowns and Dragons

First, Juliet had something important to do. On the bus ride home, she sat with Olivia. Olivia looked mad.

"I'm sorry," Juliet said. "I know you weren't taking sides with the boys."

"I wasn't," Olivia said quietly.

"I know," Juliet repeated. "And you don't have to wear pink every day. We can still play princess."

"Good," Olivia said. "I like to play princess."

Juliet and Olivia talked for the rest of the ride, just like always. Then the bus stopped at Olivia's house.

"Bye," Juliet said. Then she whispered, "I'll have a surprise tomorrow. It's about the party."

Olivia's eyes got wide. She waved and ran off the bus.

Juliet kept her idea a secret until dinner. She waited until her dad put out the food. Then she stood up.

"Mom and Dad, I have a royal decree," she said. "I want to invite the boys to my party."

Her parents looked at each other.

"That's nice, Juliet," her mom said. "Why did you change your mind?"

Juliet sat down. "I don't know." It was kind of hard to explain. She didn't want the boys to be mad at her. Plus, Jonathan was right. Her party was really fun last year. Jonathan was good at playing tag. Billy even won a prize in the dance contest. They made the party fun.

"I have a problem," Juliet went on. "I still want to have a Pink Princess Party. But not all girls like pink. And not all boys like to play princess."

Her dad nodded. "I get it. We need to make it fun for everybody."

"But I still want it to be a Princess Party," Juliet said.

"We can look in some of your princess books," her mom said. "I'm sure we'll find some ideas in there."

That's just what they did after dinner. Juliet and her mom sat at the kitchen table and looked at her favorite princess books.

The first was a book of fairy tales with lots of big color pictures. The first picture showed a castle.

"Castles are good," Juliet said. "Princesses live in castles. So do princes."

"And kings. And knights," her mom added. She wrote the word "castle" on a piece of paper.

They found even more good pictures in the book. There were knights with swords, and a big, green dragon. Juliet liked the dragon picture best.

"I know!" Juliet said suddenly. "We can

put a princess crown on the girl invitations, and a dragon on the boy invitations."

"That sounds good," her mom said. "Let's get to work."

Juliet used pink paper and cut out nine crowns. She cut one crown from yellow paper. Then she stuck each crown onto a card with a glue stick and used a glitter pen to add jewels to the crowns. They looked great!

"That's beautiful," Mrs. Henry said. "Who is the yellow one for?"

"That one's for Olivia," said Juliet. "Yellow is her favorite color."

Mrs. Henry found a picture of a dragon on the computer. She printed out ten dragons and cut them out. Juliet glued each dragon onto a card.

When she was finished, Juliet opened one of the cards. She read what was inside.

Juliet is turning 7!
Please come to her
Pink Princess Party!

"Do you like it?" her mom asked.

"I like it," Juliet said. "The dragons look good. But will the boys come to a Pink Princess party?"

"I think they will," her mom said. "Just wait and see."

Juliet put the cards in envelopes and wrote a name on each one. She saved Billy's card for last.

Would Billy come? Would he stay mad at her? Would he be a pirate and try to steal her birthday cake?

There was only one way to find out. Juliet wrote Billy's name on the card.

Her party was one week away. How could she wait so long?

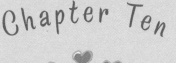

Chapter Ten

The Perfect Princess Party

"Happy birthday, Juliet!" her mom and dad called.

Juliet ran into the kitchen. The table was covered with a pink tablecloth and had a vase of pink flowers in the middle.

"Good morning, Princess," her dad said. He put a plate of food in front of Juliet. "Here are seven pink pancakes for my seven-year-old girl!"

"Thanks!" Juliet said, giggling. She put strawberries on top of her pancakes. The pancakes were the perfect size, and she ate every single one.

After breakfast, Juliet helped set up for the party. Her mom tied pink balloons to the rails on the back porch. They set up a craft table in the yard. There was cardboard and scissors and jewels and glue to make crowns. There were paper-towel rolls and silver paper for making swords.

Juliet's dad put the cake on another table. The cake looked just like a castle! It had tall towers and a wall around it. It was covered in  frosting with little pieces of pink candy stuck in it. They looked like jewels.

"It's beautiful!" Juliet said. "Do you think the boys will like it?"

"Yes, they will," her dad told her. "Plus, not all of the food is pink. Come look at this."

Juliet followed her dad into the kitchen. Mr. Henry picked up a plate with a hot dog on it. But it was not a normal hot dog. It looked like a dragon!

"Wow!" Juliet said. "How did you do that?"

"I used vegetables to make the eyes, feet, spikes, and a tail," he said. "See? The eyes are olives."

"Those are great!" Juliet cried. She was really getting excited now.

"I need to make more," Mr. Henry said. "Your party will start soon."

Juliet looked at the clock. "It's hours

away! What if everything turns back into a pumpkin before then?"

Her dad laughed. "Not to worry, Cinderella. I didn't make all this stuff with a magic wand."

While she waited, Juliet changed into her pink party dress. It had a puffy pink skirt. As the finishing touch, she put the crown on her head.

Juliet smiled and picked up Princess Allissa. "We look exactly alike, Allissa."

Juliet wasn't sure, but for a second it looked like Princess Allissa smiled right back at her.

At that moment, the doorbell rang. Juliet ran downstairs to get it. The party was about to start!

She opened the door. Billy and Jonathan were the first ones there. Billy handed Juliet a present wrapped in pink paper.

"Happy birthday," he said.

"Thanks," Juliet said. "I like the paper. But I thought you didn't like pink."

Billy pulled a pair of sunglasses out of his jeans pocket. He put them on.

"I brought these in case the pink gets too bright," he said.

Juliet laughed. She knew Billy was just joking.

"Come on in," she said.

The bell rang again and again. All of the girls and boys from Mrs. Masters's class came.

They ate dragon hot dogs and pink sandwiches. They made crowns and swords. Olivia made a yellow crown. Billy made a red crown. He stomped around the yard crying, "All hail King Billy!"

Olivia and Kristen made swords. They had a pretend sword fight.

Then everyone played tag. Juliet's mom put on music, and they danced. When it was time for cake, everyone sang "Happy Birthday!" Juliet blew out the candles and made a secret wish.

I wish every day could be a princess day!

Juliet's mom and dad hugged her before they cut the cake.

"Are you glad you invited the boys?" Mrs. Henry whispered.

"Of course," Juliet said. "You can't have a princess party *without* boys!"

Everyone was running around and having fun. Juliet stood on a chair to get their attention.

"I have a royal decree!" she said in a loud voice.

Everyone got quiet.

"What is it?" Billy called out.

Juliet smiled. "Thank you for coming to my Pink Princess Party!"

Make It Yourself!
♡ Princess Food ♡

You don't have to have a princess party to make these treats. Just like Juliet, you can make this fairy tale food and turn *any* day into a princess day!

Pink Princess Sandwich

Level of difficulty: Medium
(You'll need some help from a grown-up.)

You Need:
- 2 pieces of bread
- whipped cream cheese
- strawberry or raspberry jelly
- plastic knife
- large heart-shaped cookie cutter

1. Use the cookie cutter to cut each piece of bread into the shape of a heart. (If you don't have a heart-shaped cookie cutter, a grown-up can cut the bread with a knife.)

2. Spread the cream cheese on one piece of heart-shaped bread. Spread the jelly on the other piece. Stick the two pieces together so the cream cheese and jelly meet. Now you have a perfect pink princess sandwich! With two more slices of bread, you can make one for a friend, too.

Hot Dog Dragon

Level of difficulty: Hard
(A grown-up **must** help you.)

You Need:

- 1 hot dog
- 1 green bell pepper
- 1 red bell pepper
- some small green olives stuffed with pimentos
- 1 can of cheese snack (the kind you squirt out!)
- 1 scallion
- sharp knife
- cutting board

1. Ask a grown-up to cook the hot dog in boiling water until it is hot and juicy.

2. While the hot dog is cooking, ask a grown-up to cut up the vegetables.

♡ Cut the green pepper in half from top to bottom and lay it flat, then cut the pepper into six small triangle shapes. These will be the dragon's feet and spikes.

♡ Cut open the red pepper and lay it flat. Cut a long, thin rectangle from the pepper—no bigger than 1/4 inch wide. Cut angles into the end of the strip to make it look like the dragon's tongue.

💜 Cut a green olive into thin circles. Each circle will be green on the outside and red on the inside. These will be the dragon's eyes.

💜 Cut off most of the white bulb of the scallion. Trim the green part so it's about four inches long. Slice the green parts so they get frilly and curly. This will be the dragon's tail.

💜 Once the hot dog has cooled a bit, have a parent cut four half-inch slits, lengthwise, into the top of the hot dog. Cut two horizontal half-inch slits into each side of the hot dog. Cut a horizontal slit into each end of the hot dog.

3. Now for the best part: It's time to put together your dragon! You can do this yourself. Start by putting a green pepper triangle into the slits on the side of the hot dog. These are the dragon's feet. Next, stick a green pepper slice into each slit on top of the hot dog. These are the dragon's spikes.

4. Stick the scallion into one end of the dragon to make the tail.

5. To make the face, stick the red bell pepper slice into the slit at the other end of the hot dog to make the tongue. Then add the eyes. Use the cheese like glue to stick the olive eyes right above the tongue.

"'Once upon a time, there was a princess named Crystal,'" Isabel Dawson read out loud. "'Crystal lived in a beautiful castle.'"

Isabel looked at the picture of the castle in her book. It was made of stone and had lots of towers. Princess Crystal was looking out of a window.

"That's a nice castle," Isabel said to herself. "But it's too bad she doesn't have a *purple* castle, like mine!"

Isabel looked around her own castle and smiled. It was made out of Isabel's bunk beds! She had a room all to herself, so she only needed one bed. Isabel slept on the top bunk. Her dad had taken out the mattress on the bottom. Her mom had hung a purple curtain in front of the space. Then Isabel had filled it with everything a castle needed.

There were comfy purple pillows on the floor. A small bookshelf held Isabel's favorite books. On the top shelf, Isabel had carefully placed her collection of princess figures. They looked like tiny statues. Most of the princesses wore purple dresses, because that was Isabel's favorite color in the whole world!

Finally, her dad had attached a lamp to the wall so Isabel could read inside her castle. She loved to read—especially books about princesses. Princesses always wore beautiful clothes. They had magical adventures. And they all lived happily ever after!

Isabel's big brothers, Alex and Marco, thought she was weird for reading so much. They liked to tease her.

"Izzy is a nerd!" they would chant. "Dizzy Izzy!"

Isabel didn't mind being called a nerd.

But she *hated* being called Izzy. She couldn't imagine a princess named Izzy!

Inside her castle, Isabel felt safe. Nobody in her castle called her Izzy.

Knock! Knock! Knock!

Somebody was banging on Isabel's door.

"Go away!" Isabel yelled.

"But I have to ask you something." It was one of her big brothers, Alex.

"I'm busy!" Isabel shouted back.

She heard the door open. "Then I'll just have to storm the castle!" Alex cried.

He pulled open the purple curtain. "Ha, found you!" he yelled. He quickly grabbed a princess figure from her shelf and ran away. "Can't catch me!"

"Alex, give that back!" Isabel called. She threw down the book and raced after her brother.